A Little
Excitement

by MARC HARSHMAN
Illustrated by TED RAND

COBBLEHILL BOOKS / Dutton • New York

Text copyright © 1989 by Marc Harshman
Illustrations copyright © 1989 by Ted Rand

Library of Congress Cataloging-in-Publication Data
Harshman, Marc.
A little excitement / Marc Harshman; illustrated by Ted Rand.
p. cm.
Summary: Tired of the winter, Willie wishes for a
little excitement and, to his dismay, gets it.
ISBN 0-525-65001-6
[1. Fires—Fiction. 2. Country life—Fiction.]
I. Rand, Ted, ill. II. Title.
PZ7.H256247Li 1989b
[E]—dc19   88-32660
                                                CIP
                                                AC

Published in the United States by
E.P. Dutton, New York, N.Y.
a division of Penguin Books USA Inc.
Published simultaneously in Canada by
Fitzhenry and Whiteside Limited, Toronto
Typography by Kathleen Westray
Printed in Hong Kong
First edition   10 9 8 7 6 5 4 3 2 1

For my grandparents
M.H.

To Palmer & Louise Lewis
T.R.

Winter on Pleasant Ridge had gone on long enough. Sure, I loved sledding and snowmen, snowballs and snowforts. But they can be boring, especially when you live so far in the country that your only companions are a pair of older sisters. Half the time they didn't even want to play, and the other half when they did, they were always too bossy. Mom said maybe I was too fussy. Anyway, I was tired of winter and tired of being bossed.

And what else was there? Not much. Get up. Go out in the dark and carry hay while Dad milked. Eat. Go to school. Go home and carry hay again. Eat. Study. And put up with Annie and Sarah. Not much fun I can tell you.

Annie and Sarah would tease me about the girl that the bus driver made me sit beside. When we played games, it was always them against me, and if I cheated—just to make it fair —they complained!

Mom tried. She'd offer to play checkers and sometimes we did. But you can't tell your friends when they ask what you did last night: "Oh, played checkers with Mom." I liked working with Dad but winter wasn't the fun time for that. Winter work was all mud and buckets and cow manure. And at night after chores, Dad could only slump in his chair, too tired to do much with any of us. I wondered if he would ever get his old summer strength back.

Some days it seemed all I could wish for was that something exciting might happen. One Sunday when we visited Grandma after church, I listened to her tell about her winters as a girl. She would ride to town on a sleigh behind two black mares. There were blizzards that topped the roof of the old porch. And sometimes her school would be closed for

weeks at a time. It all sounded pretty good, and lots more exciting than my winter. But when I told her this, she said, "Be careful what you wish for, Willie, you might just get it." Well, I didn't quite understand that. I didn't see why you'd have to be careful. I thought the best thing in the world that could happen to this winter would be a little excitement.

Mom heard the strange, loud roar first. She woke up Dad and he ran down the stairs, switched on the light, and saw the glow from the overheated stove. Dad's weariness had caught up with him. When he loaded up the stove with as much wood as it could hold that cold night, he forgot to shut out the air. So, instead of burning slowly, the fire swelled white hot and ignited the tar built up inside the chimney. He hollered everyone awake, but it was Sarah who yelled at me, pulled off my covers, and stumbled beside me down the stairs. Was this what I'd wished for?

I was cold and the snow lay deep on the hill. In our pajamas we stood shivering, and in the dark at the top of the roof, out of the red brick chimney, roared a red-thick fire. Dad ran back in and closed the stove and hoped enough air would be stopped to slow the burning.

As the blaze crackled and spit above us, Dad and Annie set up the ladder and I ran for buckets. The heat from the burning tar could crack the chimney and set the house on fire inside and we couldn't do anything about that. But outside we could at least make sure the roof didn't catch fire. We broke ice on the spring and hauled up—carefully, carefully—that black water to keep the roof safe from sparks and cinders. And while that dark, moonless night was lit by the fiery torch atop our helpless house, there were no jokes but lots of "hurry-up" and silence.

Side by side with Annie I worked,
quietly and hard and quickly, to keep the
buckets coming to Dad. Later I saw his
hands bloody from fighting to keep a
hold on that slippery roof. *Roar* and
whoosh were the sounds the fire made,
and I was more scared than excited.

While we worked with the water,
Mom and Sarah braved the house to
pack what we'd need if the worst
happened, if the whole house burned.
Everyone seemed brave that night. I kept
thinking how Annie's hands must be
frozen like mine but she never said a
word.

Eventually the Piney Volunteer Fire Department gathered: Jimmy up from Adeline, and Harry from Dutch Fork, Bob from Clouston, and Dan Creary from Sleepy Creek Hollow. They all came in pickups since the pump truck was froze up solid over at Dixon's. Neighbors from across the valley and down the ridge would arrive, too, before it was over. But, of course, the first one there was Dad himself—he joked later that no one had ever been quicker than that to a fire, and if they had, he'd eat his Sunday pants.

The night was beautiful, all white and black beyond the fire. Somewhere in that black a deer must have lifted her nose from grass pawed clear of snow, looked over our way, and wondered—too smart and too quick to be scared. I felt better when I heard Jimmy and Bob, Harry and Dan shouting and

laughing, even when it seemed they shouldn't. But finally we watched the orange flames fall back until one hour after it had started, Bob Jackson shone his flashlight down the flue and announced: "She's all gone, folks! Get on in the house and get to bed." And, of course, we didn't.

The firemen and the neighbors, as well as the furniture, crowded back indoors after Bob yelled, and oh, the talk and the food—they were better than Thanksgiving. Mom got coffee, while some of the neighbor ladies laid out cookies and

a wedge of cake they had brought from home. We ate and laughed till we'd nearly forgotten it was early morning and that a little while ago we had been more scared than we knew. Annie and Sarah and I played without fussing or bossing. I figured now that maybe my fussing had earned me some of their bossing. I was going to remember how brave they were, too, and no boy should mind having brave friends, even if they are his sisters. Maybe, if the three of us put our heads together, we could even come up with our own excitement.

Sunrise came absolutely quiet to our hilltop farm. A new powder of snow had fallen sometime after we got back to sleep. The black ash and soot from the blaze had already disappeared under it. It felt good to see that everything was safe. I hoped when I saw Grandma that she wouldn't mention what she had said on Sunday. Besides, she wouldn't have to worry about reminding me. I'm not likely to forget.